and other family fantasies

Poems, lyrics and stories

by

Rob Parkinson

First published in Great Britain in 2011
by Caboodle Books Ltd
Copyright ©Rob Parkinson 2011

A catalogue record for this book is available from the British Library

ISBN 978 0956 5239 52

Illustrations and front and rear cover by Mark Spain
Page layout by Imaginary Journeys
Printed by

The paper and board used in the paperback by Caboodle Books Ltd are natural recyclable products made from wood grown in sustainable forests. The manufacturing processes conform to the environmental regulations of the country of origin.

Caboodle Books Ltd
Riversdale, 8 Rivock Avenue, Steeton, BD20 6SA
www.authorsabroad.com

For all my family,
animal and otherwise.

Acknowledgements:

The song lyrics in this book are from two CDs by Rob Parkinson, *The Wonderful Store* and *Wild Imaginings*, published by Imaginary Journeys and are included with full permission. (For further details, see back page.) All material is entirely original apart from *Will's New Suit,* which is based on a folktale, very extensively adapted and re-shaped.

CONTENTS

Poems & Lyrics

Two family tall tales

THE STORY

I'm a storyteller as much as a writer and there's more than one story in this book. Apart from the two tall tales at the end, there are also stories in some of the poems and song lyrics. There are stories in the background too, because there's quite a lot about Jay's life and then you have to imagine a lot more for yourself.

Some poems are about Jay and his family and relatives. Some are the kinds of poems that Jay himself writes and some are the kind he would write if he got round to it, all about things and people he knows. Then there are the lyrics of songs that Jay is listening to when he's imagining and thinking about themes in the poems. This may seem a bit bigheaded, but these are all by me, from some recordings I made a while ago. To be fair I have to admit that Jay could be listening to songs by a lot of other people who write much more famous songs than I do, but I'm not allowed to put their words in this book, so I've just given you mine. You can actually hear them yourself if you follow the links on the website given below. As for the other songs, maybe you already know some of them, maybe you like them too.

I don't know whether your family is like Jay's or whether you ever think and dream the same sorts of things as he does Maybe a lot, maybe a bit, maybe not at all. Jay himself is a normal kind of boy who lives a normal kind of life, has normal kinds of friends and plays normal kinds of games, though he is a bit dreamy and absent minded. The poems come from different times in his life, so I won't tell you his exact age now. He has a sister and a brother who sometimes annoy him - which is quite normal too. His mum and dad are... well, almost normal, though they're not perfect and they do have rows sometimes, which is not exactly unusual.

Families are different in some ways, the same in others. Part of family life is in the things you do and the people you see and talk to. Part of it is the dreams and fantasies you have, the stories you tell yourselves and then the feelings and the fears, which is all a bit more hidden. The poems here are about everyday things and then about just a few of the hidden things too. Anyway, you'll just have to read and see what could be the same for you and what is totally different. It's good to be nosy sometimes; it's how you find out the important things.

I'll leave Jay to introduce himself and the poems and stories. He wanted to add some more comments but we needed the space for the tall tales at the end, so you'll have to imagine what else he might have said too.

- Rob Parkinson June 2011

HI! I'M JAY. HOPE YOU'LL ENJOY THIS BOOK. I THINK IT'S COOL BUT THEN I WOULD BECAUSE I'M IN IT.

You can listen to the songs by clicking the links at
www.imaginaryjourneys.co.uk

My Dad's Not a Dog

My dad's not a dog
But he's a bit like one
When he scratches himself and yawns,
Mouth round and dark as danger,
Or when he snarls his anger
And barks and growls a warning,
Or when he does disgusting smells
And doesn't seem to care.

My mum's not a cat,
But she hisses when she's cross
And screeches when you forget things
Though, when she likes you best,
It's as if she got the cream
And wants to curl up by your fire.
Then she purrs you to sleep,
Stroking your face with hands soft as paws.

My gran is not a mole,
But sometimes she peers at me
As if she spent a long time in a hole
And is just getting used to daylight.
She's not a bird either,
But sometimes her eyes go big like an owl's
And glowing green with astonishment
At things you tell her.

My uncle is not a giraffe,
Even though he's vague and tall
And peers down at you as if his business
Is all up high and he can't recall
What it's like on the ground

And can't tune in at all
To anything you say -
It's too far down.

My aunty's not an anteater,
But her snout twitches like one
And she stiffens like a hunting creature
When she gets a sniff of news.
Her small black eyes glitter at the gossip,
As if she's licking up lots of deliciously
Tickly, wriggly little creatures
With a long pink tongue.

My grandad's not a bear,
Even though he's cuddly.
He comes out from his shed/cave,
His clothes crumpled and creased
Like fur he hibernated in,
And huffs his way into the house
And slurps his sweet tea
As if it were honey.

But now my brother and sister -
Well they prove the stuff people say
About where we come from.
It's the way they play -
The shrieks and wild giggles.
You know straight away
They're just monkeys in clothes,
Unlike me.

Dad's Music

Jay's dad's the kind who can't travel far
Without putting on the music in the car.
Nothing quiet and calm you understand;
He's into blues and metal bands
And jazz rock – old-fashioned stuff,
But cool to him and loud enough
To make your ears spin,
Though Jay's dad just loves the din.

Sometimes he thrashes the steering wheel
With that crazy drummer's crazy feel,
Or bounces like a berserk baby in his seat,
Or taps his big, black-booted feet
On the control pedals, even when you're moving,
Or jerks his head around like he's grooving
The hours away in some all night bar,
Instead of controlling an ordinary car.

Sometimes he even sings along:
Jay's dad knows strange words to strange songs.
Then he'll play air guitar at the traffic lights.
It's the kind of too embarrassing sight
You wouldn't want your friends to see -
Half hairy wild man, half bald chimpanzee.
Sometimes it makes his driving bad,
Sometimes Jay pretends it's not his dad.

Not that anyone's taken in -
Jay's dad's committed another sin:
He's just like his son; the family look's
Written plainer than a big print book.
Jay's an image of how his dad used to be;
Jay's dad's a glimpse of what Jay could be.
But in the music, they almost change places:
Dad's the kid; Jay tries on sniffy grown-up faces.

Climbing Trees

I like climbing trees,
So high, you can't see me,
So high I just be me
Climbing trees.
That's what I like.

You have to stay with it,
You have to just live it;
Your mind just rivets
On climbing trees.
That's what I like

Down is a long way
So you can't afford wrong ways;
You know it's not kid's play,
Climbing trees.
That's what I like

Mum says it's frightening,
Dad's knuckles are whitening,
But my grip is tightening
On branches and bark.
That's what I like.

You know you just learn lots
In reaching the high spots;
It's trusting yourself lots,
Just getting there.
That's what I like.

Up there there's no strife;
You feel keen as a clean knife.
I'll spend my whole life
Climbing trees.
That's what I like.

Sisters

Some sisters are stars, some are certainly not,
Some sisters are cool, some are too hot.
Some sisters care and some just don't,
Some sisters support you and some just won't.
You never quite know with sisters.

There are sisters who nibble like annoying gnats
At old wounds and resentments and ongoing spats.
They fan the flames of arguments and squabbles
And seem to like making your confidence wobble.
You never quite know with those sisters.

Some snigger when they've done something specially bad
And then put on angel faces for Dad,
Who thinks they are lovely, so sweet and so nice,
Whilst you know they're spiteful experts in vice.
They never quite know such sisters.

Other sisters make faces and whisper about you
To make sure that people will definitely doubt you
And think that you're the one in the wrong,
Whilst she is the person who's always on song.
They never quite know such sisters.

Yet some sisters sing anthems of unstinting praise
And celebrate deeds that you've done for days
And are proud of you even when you make mistakes
And help you no matter how much effort it takes.
Not everyone gets such sisters.

There are sisters who say that enough is enough
And would you please take your hands off their stuff
And it's time you set to and did your share of the chores,
After all you're not perfect and some mess is yours.
You can't always win with sisters.

Sisters are special: you'll never quite lose
The taste of them, not like the friends that you choose.
Sweetly or sourly, it goes on for ever:
They know you in ways you hope friends will never.
There's all sorts of knowing in sisters.

Some sisters are saints, some are snakes,
Some sisters ring true, some are just fakes;
Some sisters are gold and always will like you,
Some sisters go cold and filled with fight too.
You'll just have to see with your sister.

Brothers

(as seen from a bad mood)

Bury him deep in a pit, fill it with water,
Get the crocodiles and the sharks
And the snakes and the piranhas
And don't forget the giant spiders
In case he gets out, then they can finish him off.

Brotherly love? I love you like a brother?
Huh! You can keep that stuff.
Brothers are a pain and that's that -
More or less, most of the time,
Most days, most places.

Yeah, OK, there are days,
Like where there's nothing to do;
No friends around, just grown-ups.
They're useful then, sort of.
They know the right games.

And yeah, OK, there are limits.
Sharks yes, bully boys no –
You wouldn't let them have him.
They're even worse than brothers,
Just about.

And anyway, you know that pit
The one with the nasty stuff?
Yeah, right, well maybe you would shove him in,
But then in the end you'd pull him out -
At least when he was good and scared.

Mum and School

Jay's mum seems to like school.
She wants him to follow all the rules
Sit where he's told to, go where he's sent -
And she always asks him how it went.

Jay says, 'Fine!' but it's not enough;
She likes the highly detailed stuff.
'What did Mrs Smithson say?
What kinds of sums did you do today?

'How did your assembly go? Did you do well?
Who did you play with? Did anyone tell?
Did you hand in your homework? Did you give in that letter?
Did you try your best to do better and better?'

It's not something Jay wants to explain -
Frankly sometimes it's a real pain.
He'd rather go and chill out somewhere,
But she insists and he doesn't dare

To say, 'Don't be nosy. I don't want to say!'
Which he thinks sometimes after a difficult day,
Though at other times, in fact, he can't recall
A single thing he did at all,

Except wish it was Christmas or the summer holiday
And dream of being famous and play
At stuff and tell Ben he's a stupid baby,
And then get nagged by the lunchtime ladies.

Which is annoying when it's not your fault –
Ben likes making trouble. He gave Jay such a jolt
That he spilled his custard on Mr Shiner's shoes.
But he knows that's just not the kind of news

Mum wants to hear. Jay's too honest, he doesn't tell lies
About how his great genius has been recognized
At last. He repeats 'It's all fine, Mum!' hoping she'll stop
Going on about how he must get to the top.

She seems to believe that he's misunderstood -
Which might just be true: Jay knows that he could
Work harder if he felt really inspired,
But as it is right now he's just tired.

And the thing is, she sees school in a particular mum way,
Which is why she wants so much from her loved son Jay.
For her it's a big test she needs him to get through,
For Jay it's OK; it's just something you do.

The Path to School

The path to school is not the same -
It plays endless new games.
You have to stay sharp to see the ways
It makes itself different on different days,
In different disguises.

Sometimes the path is black
Like a glossy plastic rubbish sack.
You can stand on yourself in the puddles,
Balanced over a back-to-front muddle -
Right is left; left is right.

Sometimes the path is shaded
The way a morning sun disc made it,
Stretching beams over steaming slates
And greying the gardens and gates
Where they couldn't quite reach.

Sometimes the path's white
And crunches, crisp as breakfast bites.
You can read your tracks like a story
Written in the sparkly glory
Of frosted paving stones

But sometimes the path to school stinks
And there's mess that makes your heart sink,
With cans squashed like cross faces
And dark dirt streaks and bright paint traces
In angry scribbles.

Then again sometimes it seems wobbly
Where the summer heat shimmers oddly,
Zig-zagging the air into swirls
And sketching weird water worlds
You can never walk into.

And all these roads lead to just one place
That seems to put on just one face:
School – though that's not quite true,
It just seems that way to you
And everyone pretends it is.

Arthur's Space Luggage

(A monologue)

Arthur the spaceman was off on a trip,
A full year away in his silver spaceship,
Beyond the stars, through the Milky Way,
Where planets are born and comets play.

Arthur had everything worked out and planned;
The spaceship stood ready, all spick and span.
He stepped on the gangway; the watching crowd cheered.
He was going to climb in when him mum said,

'HERE! ARTHUR! HAVEN'T YOU FORGOTTEN SOMETHING?'

'Your toothbrush you'll need if I'm not mistaken
And toothpaste and soap. You really need shaking!
You'd forget your own head if it wasn't screwed on!
And whilst we're at it, you need some more food on.

'You've got to have fruit, so I brought you this crate
Of apples and pears. They're great
For your tum... Here's some ointment. Come, come!
You might get a nasty old boil on your bum.

'Here's some Mars Bars, some sweets, three good
    feather pillows,
Your teddy, your favourite fluffy pink armadillo
For comfort at night – you'll be all tucked up warm
If you're caught in a nasty old meteorite storm.'

She rushed up the gangway and gave him these things.
He had to say thank you and smile and grin,
Though with everyone there, he felt such a wally.
Then, before he could blink, she was back with a trolley.

'I brought you these comics in case you get bored...
Well it won't be all thrills and adventures I'm sure.
And some crosswords and puzzles and cards of course,
Your toy spacemen... oh, and your old rocking horse.

'Ten changes of pants, ten hankies, ten vests
And six woolly jumpers – it gets cold on star quests!
Thirty changes of socks – oh, they do get so smelly
And you know how you sweat in those dreadful space wellies.

'Now Arthur, come here! There's moondust in your eye.
I'll just get it out. There there now, don't cry!
Just look at your space boots! They're all scuffed and black!
And your spacesuit! It's all worn down the back!

'Oh well, too late now to mend it I suppose.
Which reminds me, I brought you this rose
From the garden to wear... and a few carrots...
And this picture of Grandma's stuffed parrot...'

I needn't go on - you've got the idea,
But she brought plenty more. The crowd laughed and jeered.
As Arthur just took it and stowed it inside.
When she'd finally finished, she kissed him and sighed.

He closed up the hatches, then everyone gasped
At the engine's roar and the rocket's blast.
But the spaceship stood still, it spluttered and coughed –
There was too much inside and it couldn't lift off.

Inside

When Jay goes inside his mind,
He finds pictures he didn't know were there -
Snowy wastes, deep dark forests,
Mountains, deserts, desperate soldiers,
Love and kissing (too embarrassing!),
Mists and mornings, evenings and dark.

Also a strange gate you mustn't open,
Painted the colour of questions,
And fabulous boxes inside fabulous boxes
That go on and on for ever, getting smaller,
Till you get to a light brighter than anything
Where everything merges.

His mum hasn't found this out yet –
There's no way to tell her and she's too busy.
She judges harshly: 'Jay, you're dreaming again!'
And sometimes, 'You can't eat dreams you know!'
Jay's mind says, 'Maybe - but the taste is good.'
And then, mysteriously, 'They feed you all the same.'

Just as well, though, to keep that voice quiet.
There are worlds you can't take parents to,
That they have forgotten long ago.
It's best not to upset them with reminders
Of all that they have lost,
Best to sit on the secret whilst you have it.

Parents at War

When parents start to argue,
It's best to hunker down
Like a soldier in a bunker
Dodging bullets.

Whizz! They're chucking insults
Like angry smoke grenades.
Pheeeeew! That word's too sharp -
It could have hurt!

Bang! Bazooka phrases hit their targets
And their voices are exploding.
Look out! Keep out the way!
It's dangerous round here

It's the time of temper losing
And it all gets so confusing
When they become two kids
In grown-up bodies

Hurling spears of angry words,
Clubbing hard with accusations,
Sniping with sneers
And screwed up sobs.

Do you really need this squabbling
When your confidence is wobbling
And school's on about your SATs?
Why must they have these spats?

Seems almost breaking up time
When it gets worse – it's making up time!
They're lovey-dovey, smooching,
Hugging, even kissing!

Yuck! Parents!
They take so long to grow up!

This is one of my Aunty Rosy's poems. She writes her short ones inside cards she sends you, but this is on a long sheet that is blu-tacked onto our fridge. Dad says it's what's called doggerel, which is a kind of poetry that rolls along and rhymes a lot. Apparently some people don't think it's a very good idea to write doggerel, but I reckon this says some stuff that's worth saying (even if it's a bit embarrassing) and it's easier to remember when it rhymes

Sorry.

Sorry's such a tricky word, it's hard to say it right;
If they think that you don't mean it, you could be stuck in a fight.
Which you don't sometimes, but then again at other times you do
And the thing is, when you do, making it sound true

Like when, as people say, someone's really got your goat,
And the sorry's hard and heavy, so it sticks in your throat.
And it's not that you intend making it seem at all rude,
But it slips out small and sulky and embarrassingly nude

In fact sorry's a trickster; it has a monkey gang of meanings
That leap around wildly and play with all your feelings
And jeer at you and leer at you, so you can seem so small
That you're not even able to whisper it at all.

Sure, there are some versions much easier to say
Like the sorry that means 'All right it's done. Now will you go away?'
Or the one that crows 'I may be wrong but I don't believe I'm bad.'
Or the one that sneers, 'I'm saying it, but I think you're really sad!'

Then there's sorry that insists, 'You know I'm truly right.'
And the one that shouts 'Get out my way unless you want a fight!'
Or there's sorry that spits 'I don't mean it and actually I hate you!'
And the kind that screams 'I couldn't care if they exterminate you!'

18

Or there's an over humble sorry that sighs, 'Please don't mind me',
Or a tumble over sorry that cries 'Oh *!??*!!! I didn't see!'
Or there's a mild sorry that smiles 'I'm just a bit surprised
That I've been caught behaving this little bit unwise.'

But those are cheaper sorries; there are some that cost you dear,
Like ones where pride is in the way, plus a certain kind of fear
That saying the word will makes you look the kind of stupid fool
Who never once again will be able to look cool.

Sometimes, though, such sorries lead to smiles and great big hugs,
Where you all admit, right there and then,
                                        that you've been stupid mugs
And it doesn't matter really now it's over and it's done with
And you're in a better time that this sorry is begun with.

Maybe it's what it's all about – not just putting on polite
But giving up the feelings that got you in the fight.
Which is great when it happens, though it can't always work
Since all those other sorries in the background like to lurk.

Yes, sorry is a tricky word, it's hard to say it right;
If they think that you don't mean it, you could be still stuck in a fight.
Which you don't sometimes, but then again at other times you do
And the thing is, when you do, making it sound true.

Fred the Friendly Dragon

(song lyric)

Just last year I had a dragon to stay;
He came to the door one sunny day.
He was big as a bear with bright green scales,
He'd a crest on his back and a long long tail.
He said, 'Hello! My name is Fred!'
Then he lay down by the garden shed.
I tucked him up and sang a bedtime song
And he snoozed out there the whole night long.

Dragons are good and dragons are great!
Fred the Dragon was my best mate.

When you have a dragon to stay, it's fun.
You don't need a fire or an oven or sun
Because a dragon's got fire in his great big nose,
He could warm your house with a couple of blows.
Fred breathed on bread to make my toast,
He'd warm my porridge or my Sunday roast
And when he went for his morning fly,
I'd hang my washing on his wings to dry.

Dragons are good and dragons are great!
Fred the Dragon was my best mate.

Sometimes Fred was soppy and dumb,
He'd lie on his back and I'd tickle his tum.
He'd kick his legs out, laugh and roar
Till the neighbours banged on the wall next door.
'Can't you keep that creature quiet!' they'd go.

'What is it? A rhino or a buffalo?'
'No, a dragon!' I'd shout.
'Oh, very funny! I suppose he sleeps on jewels and money?'

Dragons are good and dragons are great!
Fred the Dragon was my best mate.

But then one day, the news got out -
Fred was spotted on a walkabout.
They came and took some film for the telly
With me astride his soft white belly.
But when they asked about his hoard,
Fred snorted smoke, he roared and roared.
'I won't tell you!' I heard him say
As he smashed their cameras and flew away.

Dragons are good and dragons are great!
Fred the Dragon was my best mate.

I must not say where Fred has gone -
You might talk and pass it on.
He could be floating on a cloud
Or snoring on his hoard deep underground.
But if you meet him, treat him right -
He likes a dragon story every night
And he'll do exactly what he's told,
Unless you ask about his gold

Dragons are good and dragons are great!
Fred the Dragon was my best mate.

Jay's Creatures

Jay keeps a unicorn inside his mind;
Also a dragon, a griffin, a centaur and other
Mythical beasts people say don't exist.

If he tunes in, he can sense them superbly:
The silver-gold gleam of hide and hoof,
The snout fire with its sulphur stink.

They're as real as silk-soft cats and dancy dogs
You might stroke and fuss and pet,
More real than cows seen from car windows.

You have to close your eyes to get them
Instead of glimpsing them through glass;
You have to shut out the usual world.

If you keep them closed, you can ride the unicorn,
Count the dragon's hoard, talk conundrums with the centaur
And go on surprising adventures.

Sometimes Jay can be flying high, even in a lesson.
Sometimes they do his homework with him
Or learn the sums in tests.

It's better than a DVD or a Nintendo game.
They're fun, but it's not the same,
More unplanned. No one else gets it your way.

Having untamed acres in your head is good
Except at night when the monsters come out.
Also the witches, scrawny and cracked and crazy.

You don't ask them in but they come all the same
And then they threaten to stay.
It takes time to make the bargain with them.

When at last you get to know how,
They'll vanish leaving true treasure.
But that takes skill. Jay's working on it.

Hoody Hag

My hoody hangs
On a hook
On the back
Of my bedroom door.

Sometimes in the night,
In the half light
Cast by the hall light,
It looks ghostly
Or worse,
Like a twisted hag.
Wicked as a curse.

Once I thought I saw it move.
I stayed awake all night
Hidden under the duvet.

Imagination Masters

Domi's dogs loomed out of dreams,
Big as bears, with teeth like cutlasses.
A real one bit him once; after that
Things canine crept into his head
In scary new disguises every night.
In the day, it was no use saying
Most dogs are friendly -
You can't take chances with beasts that bite.
Even Yorkshire terriers fazed him;
Wolfhounds and St Bernards were hell on legs.

Imagination masters fixed it.
Made this magic film you could control.
Dogs capered, squirmed and even danced,
Then turned small as beetles;
You could tame them, stroke their soft, sad tummies.

For Corrina it was corners, dark ones.
You never knew what would be there -
Beasts, boggarts or burglars,
Poisonous snakes or sinister soldiers
On a mission to destroy the house.
Sneering supply teachers,
Daunting dinner ladies,
Bouncing bullies or leaping lions:
Her mind could conjure them all
And then some more.

Imagination masters took her through a dark
So thick you'd trip over it,
Gave her a light inside, a clever trick
That shone away the shadows
And was always there.

Ghosts haunted Guy when he was alone,
Murderers hid under Michael's bed
Whilst Vicky's sense of dread
Even cuddles couldn't cure:
It chilled her to the core.
Sophie was never helped
By dad saying it was crazy
To let your fancy make such silly pictures;
A giant peanut always seemed to stalk her
In the middle of the night.

Imagination masters knew the trick
To make them pack their bags and go.
Now there's no one under the bed,
The peanut's vanished, the ghosts have given up
And Vicky's warm inside without a single hug.

Fears lurk in mind corners, waiting to mug you.
You never know which one will get through -
Mice or rats or crawly creeps,
High places, tunnels, flying, drowning,
Being locked up in a big black box
Or wearing frilly pyjamas to school,
Or just being made to look like a geek
Or being nominated as nerd of the week.
They like to hijack your imagination:
That's the way in.

But imagination masters know the score.
They turn them round, turn them back.
Imagination, they'll tell you, is a curse or a gift,
It depends how you use it.
That's the secret.

It's the Bungool

(Song lyric)

When you walk all alone in the dark,
Out in the midnight air,
You might hear a nasty noise in the dark
And feel that you had better beware.
It could be an ugly troll with three heads
Or a grumpy old giant who likes human sandwich spread,
Or a ghost or a ghoul or a teacher from your school
But it's not!

It's the BUNGOOL! That's what it is,
As he creeps just out of sight!
It's the BUNGOOL! That's what it is
And he just can't get it right.

When you wake in the middle of the night,
There's a creaking on the stairs.
You'd like to get up and turn on all the lights,
But you can't because you're terribly scared.
It could be a six foot thirty stone gorilla
Or a vampire who thinks it's time for her dinner,
Or a boggart or a bogey or the phantom of a fogey
But it's not!

It's the BUNGOOL! That's what it is
As he creeps just out of sight!
It's the BUNGOOL! That's what it is
And he just can't get it right.

When the Bungool wants to scare you,
He will try day after day,
So determined to nightmare you
That he gives himself away.

Listen to that awful crash
And the chilling howls and wails!
Bungool's tripped on his own moustache
And tangled with his tail.

So if you see a shadow in the gloom
And something brushes your face,
No need to hide in the corner of the room
Nor get inside an empty suitcase.
It could be a witch concocting a spell
Or a hairy great demon come to drag you off to hell,
Or a leopard or a lion or even Frankenstein,
But it's not! IT'S THE BUNGOOL!

Winston & the Wolves

(Song lyric)

Winston heard the wolves in the kitchen one night
When his mum & dad were fast asleep.
Their barks and their howls woke him up in a fright
And made his flesh start to creep.
But he plucked up his courage and he walked downstairs -
It made him angry to think of them there.
And there they were with red eyes all big:
Six wild wolves stealing goodies from the fridge.

Wolves can be wicked, wolves can be wild,
But wild wicked Winston has the wolf taming style.

If Winston was frightened, well it just didn't show,
Maybe he'd a natural knack.
He raised his hand and he just shouted, 'NO!'
And those wolves just froze in their tracks.
They stood stone still with pink tongues lolling out,
With crumbs in their fur and cream on their snouts:
Six magic wolves all ready to obey,
Six dream wolves all ready to play.

Wolves can be wicked, wolves can be wild,
But wild wicked Winston has the wolf-taming style.

'Come on!' said Winston, and they went outside
And Winston fetched out his sledge.
He yoked them up like huskies and then, 'Mush!' he cried
And those wolves just flew over the hedge.
They went high over the houses with the town far below,
With Winston clinging on wondering where they'd go.

That night they took him to the moon and back
And to wild strange places on the wolf wild track.

Wolves can be wicked, wolves can be wild,
But wild wicked Winston has the wolf-taming style.

Now every night, Winston rides through the sky,
Those wolves go fast enough!
Winston has trained them so they fly really high
And find him treasure and stuff.
His mum sometimes complains about the state of the fridge
And Winston takes the blame and says his appetite's too big.
Of course he never says exactly where he's been -
It's too hard to explain and she might just scream!

Wolves can be wicked, wolves can be wild
But wild wicked Winston has the wolf-taming style.

Gregory's Ghoul

(song lyric)

Gregory's ghoul lived in the cupboard,
Nobody knew that it was there
Apart from Greg, who had discovered
Ghouls do what you say once they're outstared.
Gregory ruled that ugly old ghoul,
Though it was twice his own size
With a huge and hairy nose,
Sharp claws on all its toes
And big red luminous eyes.

Gregory's ghoul, Gregory's ghoul,
The ugliest of uglies was Gregory's ghoul.

If Gregory went walking in the dark,
He'd take the ghoul along on a lead
And vampires that were lurking in the park
Would scream and fly away at great speed.
Witches and ghosts would hide behind posts,
Goblins that were nasty and cruel
Were terribly scared
And none of them dared
To tangle with Gregory's ghoul.

Gregory's ghoul, Gregory's ghoul,
The ugliest of uglies was Gregory's ghoul.

Simon was a big fat bully,
Thought that he would push Greg around.
Poked him in the eye and thought it funny
Until he heard a growling sound.

The hideous ghoul that Gregory ruled
Picked up Simon, swung him by the ears.
Then he biffed him and he bopped him
And, when finally he dropped him,
Simon's hair stood on end for a year.

Gregory's ghoul, Gregory's ghoul,
The ugliest of uglies was Gregory's ghoul.

When it was time to go to sleep,
Gregory would put the ghoul to bed
And help him count ghoulish sheep
And stroke the stubbly hairs on his head.
The ghoul's noisy snores shook all of the floors
But Gregory had beautiful dreams,
Because even nightmares
Never crept up his stairs
With Gregory's ghoul on the scene.

Gregory's ghoul, Gregory's ghoul,
The ugliest of uglies was Gregory's ghoul.

Laying down the law

When Dad lays down the law,
It's best not to say a thing.
He likes to hold court
Like some bossy ancient king –

You know, the kind in those old tales
Where it's, 'Off with his head!'
For some minor kind of failure
Or just for something that you said?

'Point A,' he says and thumps the table,
'You're wrong Point B, I'm right!
That's how it is! End of fable!
Now, go to bed! Good night!'

There's no point in trying to argue -
Dad likes to think he's strict
And if you decide to try to,
He gets angry much too quick

And he turns into some other bloke
You wouldn't want to know.
It's really no joke
When Dad's gorilla self's on show.

He roars and rants and shouts too
And gets in such a rage
You want to go and tell the zoo
To put him in a cage.

You can tell he's angry with himself;
He loathes these shouting fits.
He hates to hear himself
Sounding like some grumpy git

From a cartoon or a comedy,
The kind that growls and barks
Like the first pair of teachers on the day
They roared out of the ark.

So best enter a plea for mercy
And let him think he's boss.
Let him be Pompous King Percy
Then perhaps he won't get cross.

After all it's always been the way
The best rebels like to follow,
To think their private thoughts today
And find their own way tomorrow.

On getting told off

I've never liked getting told off.
I mean, well why should I?
It isn't good to have them stare
With those hard, wooden eyes
And tell you you're an idiot
Or something worse
That includes some words
I won't put in this verse.

The thing is, yes I make mistakes
And so I guess that you do,
But why the big loud blaming,
Why that hocus-pocus voodoo
Where you have to play the part
And show you that you're ashamed
And wouldn't even contemplate
Doing it again?

Because in fact you would - or might:
Sometimes you just can't stop it,
Then sometimes you just feel wicked
And you reckon you can hop it
Before they catch you at it.
Go on, own up! You know you've had the thought
That the sorry they force from you just means
'I'm sorry I was caught!'

Of course, they have a point,
I suppose I'd give them that.
If I nick all the biscuits
Then I'll end up getting fat.

And there are other things I've done
That are further up the scale
Of naughtiness and not-niceness -
Not bad enough for jail

But all the same, they're wrong,
I know. You don't need to say
And the only thing I can do
Is be more right today.
So the thing is, how's it help
To make me hang my head?
Wouldn't it be better
To rehearse the good instead?

And besides they say forbidden fruit
Will always taste the best
And that's the trouble isn't it?
I don't want to get you in a mess,
But do you reckon it's possible
To avoid some tiny crimes?
Would life be so much better
If you were good all the time?

ANOTHER OF AUNTY ROSY'S POEMS FITS IN HERE. SHE SAID SHE WAS TRYING TO BE CLEVER BY NOT USING RHYMES WHEN YOU EXPECT THEM. ACTUALLY I SUPPOSE THAT IS QUITE CLEVER, THOUGH I DON'T KNOW WHAT RHYMES YOU'RE SUPPOSED TO EXPECT. I DON'T KNOW WHETHER I GET THE BIT AT THE END ABOUT COOKING EITHER. DO YOU?

Being Wrong

Being wrong is not a taste I like –
It's nasty and it's bitter;
It's very hard to swallow too;
I'd rather just be right.

That's what's supposed to feed you -
The taste of right is better.
I open my mouth to eat it
And wrong slips in instead.

I suppose I make a meal of it,
Since pride's my bread and butter.
And I guess it's pride that makes it hurt,
It's so annoying.

And often you don't want to have
Your mistakes admitted.
You'd rather make out that you're right
Or blame another person.

Owning up is like the yucky stuff
You eat when you have to,
But you'd really rather spit it out
Or leave it on the plate

Or chuck it in the bin of course -
If only you could do that
And being wrong were thrown away,
Then you'd be perfect.

Except that people don't like don't like those
Who always have the answer
And swagger round fat and full,
Like dogs who stole the dinner.

Except ... well, some good meals I've cooked
Were mistakes I turned around.
Like this poem – it's not the best chef's stuff
But wrong might make it taste right.

Being right

(Jay's rap)

You can sail the seven seas,
You can climb the highest trees,
You can pay the biggest fees,
It might seem it's all a breeze,
But you can get down on your knees
Because it's hard cheese:
And I'm right and you're wrong!
And I'm right and you're wrong!
And I'm right and you're wrong!
And I'm right and you're wrong!

You must kiss my shoes,
Bow down if I choose.
Someone's got to lose
And that loser is you.
It might give you the blues
But I'll write it in the news

That I'm right and you're wrong!
And I'm right and you're wrong!
And I'm right and you're wrong!
And I'm right and you're wrong!

My gain is your loss,
You can go and get lost!
Now I've won the toss
I really am the boss;
I don't care if you're cross,
I don't care about the cost.
I'm right and you're wrong!
And I'm right and you're wrong!
And I'm right and you're wrong!
And I'm right and you're wrong!

THAT'S IT!

Raunchy Relatives

They say Uncle John went out in the nude,
Not a stitch on, down the street for a dare
Once when he was just thirteen
And got away with it – no one caught him.

Aunty Beth, they say, was a wild child
Who danced all night in a trance
And had chucked a hundred boyfriends
Before she left school and couldn't care less.

Then there was Dan, Uncle Pete's mate,
Who climbed the statue in the middle of town
And put pink-spotted knickers on the horse's head
And left them - they were there for a week.

As for Jay's parents, well they won't say
Whether it was pranks or wicked tricks
Or what, but from their smirks,
You can tell it was bad – but fun.

To see them now, dozing on the sofa,
It's hard to believe they ever were young,
But the past had different laws
So you never know - it could be true.

Maybe trees truly were tall as the sky –
You could climb them and sit on the clouds.
Maybe you really could escape all day long
And they wouldn't send out the search parties

From what they say, you needed to sometimes.
They didn't have human teachers those days
But ogresses with steel wool for hair,
Tartan skirts and thick brown stockings.

Their punishments were cruel and dangerous;
They hung you from the blackboard,
Then pelted you with chalk
Before whacking you with a big stick.

Justin's dad says this is definitely true,
Though he also claims to be one hundred and two
When you know he's the usual fat forty-something.
Anyway Aunty Kay says no - but it felt like that.

She also says a huge snake once came into the class
And Miss Tompkins (a fierce ogress two hundred years old)
Had to call Mr Welks, the caretaker, whose beard was long
  as your arm
And who wore glasses thick as conch shells.

He wrestled with it for an hour, then called the zoo
And they came and had trouble too,
But eventually they bagged it and put it in a cage
Where it lived until two thousand and two.

These mangled myth bits they sometimes mention
Seem muddled as mad dreams, but somehow
They cling on, these bits of fantasy fluff:
Jay sees the family through a fiction filter.

I USED TO PLAY WITH LUCY QUITE A LOT WHEN WE WERE YOUNGER. SHE'S MY COUSIN AND SHE'S NEARLY THE SAME AGE AS ME. I STILL LIKE HER BUT YOU KNOW HOW IT IS. THESE DAYS MOST OF HER FRIENDS ARE GIRLS AND MOST OF MINE ARE BOYS. I SUPPOSE WE'RE JUST INTERESTED IN DIFFERENT THINGS, THOUGH WE DO LIKE SOME OF THE SAME MUSIC. I ALSO KNOW FLO, BUT SHE'S NOT MY AUNTY AND LUCY KNOWS HER BETTER. FLO DOESN'T GIVE ME PRESENTS, BUT ONCE MY NAN GAVE ME THIS PINK AND PURPLE HOODY THAT I ABSOLUTELY REFUSED TO WEAR, SO I KNOW HOW LUCY FEELS.

Clothes presents.

Aunty Flo said, 'Here's a present. It's clothes!'
Ignoring the fact that Lucy loathed
Such gifts. Flo's ideas were out of date,
Years and years and years too late,
But she always thought that what she'd bought
Was 'fashionable' or 'fun' and Lucy ought
To really love her clothes presents.

For example, there was that lacy dress
That made Lucy look a frumpy mess,
Or the waistcoat with the frothy frills,
Or the lurid lime green woolly to 'stave off winter chills',
Or the orange plastic raincoat to wear in wettest weather,
Or the tarty tartan hat with the bright yellow feather
That Flo got her as clothes presents.

This time it was school uniform, though not the normal kind
But a version from a catalogue she looked at all the time.
The colour of the cardigan was just that bit strange
And the cut of the tunic was just that fraction changed.
Flo said that it was 'stylish'. Lucy knew that it was weird
And wearing it at school would make other kids jeer
And make fun of her in her clothes presents.

Flo is not a real aunt. She's a special older lady
Who never had a family but always has loved babies.
She and Lucy's mum are friends; she often likes to call.
In fact, she looked after Lucy a lot when she was small,
So she thinks that now she knows exactly what Lucy needs,
Even though Lucy's much older now and actually she'd
Rather do without these clothes presents.

But the thing is that's a secret; it's not something she will say.
She's sensitive. Lucy knows that would ruin Flo's day
And make her feel quite sad and not like her life so much.
For Flo, buying things for people is just such
An important thing that Lucy is prepared
To look silly wearing stuff other kids wouldn't dare -
Though only once, just to thank Flo for her clothes presents

People watching

My window gives a good view
For people watching.
It's not just being nosy.

Sometimes, it's true,
You catch them scratching
Or doing something daft.

Sometimes too
They're cross and bossy
And it makes you laugh.

But other times you see them smile
And put away the angry files.
That makes it worth it

And you do learn:
No one's perfect.

The parents' game.

What is it with family grown-ups?
What are they trying to do?
Why don't they just own up
And stop playing games with you?

I mean, really, do you need it -
That slurpy, sloppy kiss,
Just when your friends can see it.
Couldn't they resist?

Or how about that little trick
Where they have to lick a hanky
And scrub and rub your face with it,
Claiming you're all manky?

Or when they talk well loud enough,
So it's almost like a cheer,
And they say the most annoying stuff
That everyone can hear?

And then they go and tell your mates
About stupid things you've done,
And fetch out your baby portraits -
They seem to think that's fun.

But even worse: them dancing!
Wiggling their butts around,
And, even though they can't sing,
Making strange strangled sounds

I'll tell you what it is: a plot!
They're all of them the same;
They 're all in it, the whole lot:
The embarrassing parent game.

There's only one way to beat 'em
And make a good show out of it.
It's the best way to treat 'em:
Ignore it. They might grow out of it.

Time Wasters

If irritating parents is your wicked aim,
There are lots of entertaining games
You can play with them just to make them mad
Without them even knowing that you've been bad.
You could get them really cross, so they start to do some shouting.
It's a lot better than going on a stupid shopping outing
When you know some time wasters

For example, know that game where you have to hunt a treasure?
Well, here's one like it that could give you some cruel pleasure,
Though you must do the hiding when they don't have
 too much leisure,
When there's a panic on and time that's left is limited and measured.
It's a game that needs all that, as you'll maybe see
When I tell you that the game I mean is called *Hunt the Key*.
It's a perfect one, a genuine time waster.

Parents love to play it, it's a tense and gripping game
And it gives them a great chance to play another one called *Blame*
Where they argue about whose fault it is that the key is lost
And nag about how much this whole thing is going to cost
Because they're late, though whilst they're at it,
You could do that one where they have to let a cat or dog in,
Then out, then in again — an excellent time waster.

Find the end of the Sellotape - that's another good one.
It could take several minutes - such pure, frustrating fun!
A very good small way to get them in a grumpy mood
And start to say some words that are likely to be rude,
The sort the teacher says are wrong, though don't ever forget

Some teachers are parents too and their own children get
Them with the same tricks: time wasters.

Knocking in the car - I suppose that does take some skill
To convince them that the engine is about to become ill.
Then there's *Threading needles* – usually best to ask a dad
Who's not good at it, then you can watch his sad
Efforts with a smirk. Or there's wire or string
Or straps that you got in a knot. *Untangling* is just the thing
To wind them right up tight with a time waster.

Last minute homework - just pretend you've forgotten
That you had to do it. Yes, I know it's a rotten
Thing to do, but of course your parents love it,
Especially when they discover that you shoved it
To the bottom of the bag all creased and screwed up
So they have to iron it flat before they can serve your food up,
Cursing to themselves about your time wasters.

There are so many of them, those are just a few.
Now here's an extra list – I'll leave it up to you
What you do with it – except... well, just don't leak it!
Whatever else happens, you must keep this poem secret,
Otherwise they might discover that I put you up to it.
They mustn't know that I or you or anyone planned how to do it.
Just make them think they're unexpected time wasters.

So

Linger on landings and dither in doorways,
Always insist upon doing things your way,
Never be ready when it's time to go
Except when they're not, then tell them they're slow.

Answer the phone and pass on those nice salesmen,
Tell them they're old if their memory fails them,
Don't pass on messages, just muddle them up,
Smash off the handle of Dad's favourite cup.

Get fluff from the carpet on your best dark clothes,
Chop off the blooms from their favourite rose,
Never admit you've done anything wrong,
Tell them they're sad when they go on and on.

Jumble up papers and hide all the cheques,
Giggle and smirk when you hear the word 'sex',
Turn up your nose when they cook something new,
Say it's like sick and tastes just like poo.

When you're bored you
Could think of more too.
I assure you
It's a cinch to
Find such time wasting, frustrating, irritating things
To make parents feel
So bad!

SECRET NOTE:

I'M NOT SUPPOSED TO TELL YOU THIS, AS ROB MIGHT GET IN TROUBLE WITH OTHER PARENTS, BUT I SHOULD ADMIT THAT HE ACTUALLY WROTE A LOT OF THIS LAST ONE FOR ME, I'M NOT QUITE SURE WHY. HE SAYS SOME OF THE GAMES ARE ONES HE SPOTTED HIS DAUGHTER PLAYING WITH HIM A WHILE AGO AND SOME ARE ONES HE'S NOTICED OTHER CRAFTY CHILDREN ENJOYING. HE ALSO SAYS THE LAST BIT IS MODELLED ON A FAMOUS SONG CALLED 'MY FAVOURITE THINGS' AND THAT YOU COULD SING IT TO THE TUNE. I DON'T THINK IT CAN BE VERY FAMOUS BECAUSE I'VE NEVER HEARD OF IT. IT'S PROBABLY SOME REALLY ANCIENT ONE THEY DID ABOUT A HUNDRED YEARS AGO.

When Gran died

When Gran died, it was sad.
Confusing too, but I couldn't say:
It wasn't allowed and they were too busy.
They said I'd understand in time,
But dying's a puzzle for everyone,
So why should I?

Flowers are beautiful - I saw it that day:
There were so many. They come and go
Like marvellous moments. It's all
Things that happen and then don't,
Like Gran too I suppose,
Like laughs and sobs.

There were two funerals -
They had another chapel next door.
I didn't care about the other one,
Though I could tell they did.
They all looked solemn for someone else,
Not my gran, not the box my family sent away.

Sometimes now I hear her speaking,
Like she's giving me advice:
She understands everything I feel.
I see her face and it's wrinkled but it's smiling.
She seems to tell me that it doesn't matter.
I don't know if it's real, but it works.

48

Pandora's Potion

(Song lyric)

Pandora was a wizard with the chemicals and such.
She'd made hair-restorer, wart remover, cures for failing sight
And some stuff for killing fleas with,
But the thing she was most pleased with
Was the potion that she made one Friday night.

She got it all worked out and she planned each last detail;
She knew what she expected it to do.
So she fixed it and she mixed it,
Then she sniffed it. When she whiffed it...
Poo! Just like old socks, a foul, unpleasant brew!

Pandora's potion, it's a dangerous notion,
Shape shifter's lotion, that's Pandora's potion.

Still she knew she'd have to taste it, she didn't want to waste it,
So she took a spoon and had a little sip.
Phew! Forget your pepper pot!
This stuff was really hot.
The tears streamed from her eyes; it burned her lip.

But a moment after that, the potion took effect
And purple hair just bushed out of her ears.
There were horns upon her head
And her skin turned green and red;
She had claws and big long fangs and a beard.

Pandora's potion, it's a dangerous notion,
Shape shifter's lotion, that's Pandora's potion.

Now Pandora was the monster that she'd sometimes been inside
And she knew exactly what she wanted next.
That chocolate cake her mum had kept
Locked away from her - she leapt

Straight through the larder door and scoffed it all.

Next she chased her brother Dave till he raved to be saved,
Then she fixed her little sister who was a nifty little twister,
Then she scared her cousin Rob who was a rotten sort of snob,
Then she frightened Aunty Mabel till she hid under the table,
Then she tickled Uncle Dick till he kicked his friend called Nick,
She even spooked the bogeyman
who had spooked her dear old gran.

She scared the teacher and the preacher
who denounced this evil creature
And the riders from police forces who chased her on their horses
And a general from the army who was posh and rather smarmy
And the soldiers with the tank who had come to stop this prank
And the aeroplanes with rockets that she caught in her side pockets.
It was impossible to stop this beast, PANDORA!

Pandora's potion, it's a dangerous notion,
Shape shifter's lotion, that's Pandora's potion.

Well it was in the news, they said it must have been an alien
Or a fierce creature not yet known to man.
No one guessed it was this daughter
So they never ever caught her.
She's normal now - with slightly hairy hands.

But Pandora now and then disappears for a while
And I don't know what she's mixing in the shed.
She looks as innocent as cream
But, knowing where this girl has been,
Maybe you'll keep away from Pandora!

Pandora's potion, it's a dangerous notion,
Shape shifter's lotion, that's Pandora's potion.

I LIKE IMAGINING HAVING ALL SORTS OF POWERS — SUCH AS MAGIC AND FLYING CARPETS OR HAVING SPECIAL DRINKS THAT CAN CHANGE YOU, LIKE PANDORA'S POTION. BUT SOMETIMES I THINK THAT MAGIC IS NEARER. IN MY PETS FOR EXAMPLE. ANYWAY, MY DOG CERTAINLY THOUGHT HE'D FOUND A MAGIC POTION.

Our dog rolled in poo

Our dog rolled in poo last week.
You should have heard my mum shriek
When he came back and she smelt the smell.
Talk about a bat out of hell!
She screamed and grabbed him by the scruff.
He looked confused — she's not normally rough.
She hauled him upstairs and put him in the bath.
I have to admit we did have a laugh,
Seeing him hating all the lady scents and foam
And probably wishing he'd never come home.

Our dog had rolled in that poo with pure pleasure.
You could tell he thought he'd found dog treasure
And that we truly would enjoy the smell too;
He wasn't expecting that stinky shampoo
My mum put on him, nor her wild shouts
Every time he struggled and tried to jump out.
She had this really fierce look on her face;
She was determined to wash off every last trace.
He writhed and wriggled and whimpered and whined.
No good — she wasn't letting him off this time.

Our dog rolled in poo and, you know, I could see
It's not the same to him as it is to me.
To me it smelt so bad that it made me feel sick,
To him it's just the kind of stuff he likes to lick.

He couldn't understand why Mum called him a fool,
He thought he smelt as lovely and stylish and cool
As she does when she's had her hair done
And puts on her best clothes to go and have fun.
It's strange to think the world's that odd:
It's one thing to us; something different to a dog.

Our dog rolled in poo. It just proves
That he and we live in quite different grooves
Within a world that looks the same.
It's a weird, peculiar and very different game
If you're a dog – he smells and hears things
Beyond my understanding.
I'm not sure we even see anything the same way -
It's just not something anyone can say.
Dogs are strange really. They share your life with you
And then they go and roll in poo.

My cat sleeps a lot

My cat sleeps a lot. She's always at it -
Upstairs or downstairs, even in our attic,
In the garden curled up in the grass,
Or on the sill behind hot window glass.
It's not just sofas, beds and chairs -
You name it, she probably sleeps there.
I even found her curled up on a towel

In the bath. It makes you wonder how
She chooses and then why.

You might think that it's just chance,
But it's a skill, like people who dance
And know exactly where the beat's at:
She can spot a sleep space just like that.
She'll sharpen her white claws to perfection,
Mew for food, eat it, start stretching
And then she's off, you don't know where
She's going to make the next secret lair,
Wherever, why ever.

When she was a kitten, it wasn't so much sleep
As pouncing, chasing, doing salmon leaps.
You thought she'd one day reach the sky,
But now she doesn't need to try.
She's done that. There's new sky to touch
In a world of dreams that's much
More fascinating to her mind
Than anything in our world and time.
That's why she sleeps a lot.

In dreams, I reckon, she rules.
It's not a country for us, we're fools
Who only think we're the bosses
Because sometimes her royal path crosses
Ours when her body needs food.
Then she pretends to be small so's not to seem rude.
Really she's a queen with huge powers.
In that world where she spends most of her hours
Seeming to sleep a lot

Cary's Candybars

(Song lyric)

Have you seen the big long queues?
Everyone's buying them, they're really good news!
They'll change your life in a minute or two,
They're wonderful, marvellous and incredible too!
If you're weedy and you're weak,
Well you could be strong and sleek!
If you're ugly and you're spotty,
There's no need to be so grotty!
You could fly to the moon and back
On the power of a single pack
Of Cary's Candybars.

Cary's Candybars, the snappiest snack you've ever tasted!
Cary's Candybars, they're absolutely great!

I'll tell you how these bars are made,
With jumping beans and lemonade
And tigers' breath and best bed springs,
All ground up with jewels and things
Like raspberries and rocket fuel,
The whoosh of wings and witches' gruel,
Fruity frothy fresh milkshake
And chunks of chewy chocolate cake.
You whisk them for an hour or two
Then you bake them in an upturned igloo
And you've got Cary's Candybars!

Cary's Candybars, the snappiest snack you've ever tasted!
Cary's Candybars, they're absolutely great!

So if you see a big fat man
Bouncing as high as a furniture van,
If you see a minute mouse
Lifting up a huge high house,
Or a wimp in winter woollies
Making mincemeat of three bullies,
Or a bonny bouncing baby
Beating up big brawny ladies,
Or a fox on a flying trapeze,
Or a hippo skipping over the seas,
They've had Cary's Candybars!

Cary's Candybars, the snappiest snack you've ever tasted!
Cary's Candybars, they're absolutely GREAT!

More More Mogey

(song lyric)

Joanna found Mogey near the park one day,
Trapped under some chucked out bricks.
This furry little creature soon began to play
And show her some incredible tricks.
It could jump into the air
Doing somersaults everywhere
And balance on the overhead wires,
Juggle thirty balls
And not let one fall
And dance just like a flame in a fire.

More, more, Mogey! Amazing and incredible Mogey!
More, more, Mogey! For Mogey is a wonderful sight!

Joanna kept the Mogey in the garden shed
And told no one about it for days.
On sugar lumps and jam this little creature fed
And the cheering and clapping and praise.
Its fur was bright red,
It had a monkeyish head
And ears like table tennis rackets;
Bright blue eyes full of charm,
Two legs and four arms
And a smile that lit up like a rocket.

More, more, Mogey! Amazing and incredible Mogey!
More, more, Mogey! For Mogey is a wonderful sight!

Now a secret like a Mogey is too hot to hold,
Soon she told a couple of friends.
They were so impressed that soon the papers were told
And hundreds came to see it in the end.

They put on a special show
To which anyone could go
And Mogey performed for the crowd,
Doing incredible feats
No one else could repeat.
Soon the cheers were long and loud.

More, more, Mogey! Amazing and incredible Mogey!
More, more, Mogey! For Mogey is a wonderful sight!

But I forgot to tell you one important thing;
Joanna didn't see it at first.
Mogeys get bigger as the cheers begin,
For praise they have terrible thirst.
Mogey grew and grew
With every trick he'd do
Until he was huge as a hangar.
Then people got scared
And ran about everywhere
Until Mogey disappeared with a BANG!

They said that Mogey was a monster
And Joanna was a freak,
She'd played a nasty trick on them all.
It was just a horrid dream
They would forget next week,
A trick for which they would not fall.

Though they said she was mad,
What made Jo really sad
Was the losing of her very best friend.
She searched everywhere,
Feeling worried and scared,
It all seemed such a sudden end.

More, more, Mogey! Amazing and incredible Mogey!
More, more, Mogey! For Mogey was a wonderful sight!

If you want to know how she found that Mogey again,
Well, it's a rather secret thing,
But there's a cave underground where you might find
    her friend
Where there's treasure that's fit for a king.
Now it lives down there
And she visits it there
And it gives her gold and teaches her stuff.
She'll never show it to you,
She's learned a lesson or two.
Mogey's small again but quite big enough.

More, more, Mogey! Amazing and incredible Mogey!
More, more, Mogey! For Mogey is a wonderful sight!

So if you find a Mogey for yourself one day,
Be careful, try to be most strict.
Don't give it too much praise or it just might not stay
And show you all its wonderful tricks.
It could teach you to fly
Or stand on the sky
If you keep it to a sensible diet.
Don't show it to the crowds
Nor cheer too loud
Or else you could be in for a riot!

More, more, Mogey! Amazing and incredible Mogey!
More, more, Mogey! For Mogey is a wonderful sight!

Muddle and Mess

I'm Muddle and this is my mate, Mess.
You don't know we're here.
We hide in corners, waiting for the chance
to creep out when you're having fun.
Then we sneak around your house
chucking stuff around,
scattering crumbs, spilling sticky drinks
and hiding vital things
where you'd least expect to find them.

The real fun thing is when you get told off.
It's great knowing that we did it
but you're getting all the blame.
You should see the hurt look on your face!
We smirk at each other when you can't explain;
we chuckle and we giggle – it's so good
seeing you wonder how it could have happened.
Well, now you know,
but of course they'll never believe you.

Sometimes we bring in Tangle -
She's good with strings and wires;
and Dirt - he's a slob.
Greasy Marks is a wild child
who jumps up on the walls or the windows
and Scribble's good at wallpaper and books.

59

Or there's Cracks and Smashes and Bangs -
they arrive along with Complete Chaos
when we're having a real party.

So that's how it works. You can't beat us.
We're always there, waiting to get through,
past all those nice little promises you make.
We know, see? We know you like us.
No use pretending; we've seen your smiles
and heard you whooping it up
when you're in the middle of those games.
You keep sending us invitations like that.
We're very polite, so we accept.

Comfort Creature

Know that feeling:
You're just there;
Nothing matters?
Know that feeling:
You're into
Whatever wherever?

Could be a game,
Could be work,
Could be a drawing,
Could be a show,
Could be a chat,
Could be a lull,
Could be with friends,
Could be alone,
Could be at school,
Could be at home,

Could be in town,
Could be at a beach,
Could be indoors,
Could be silent,
Could be singing,
Could be just staring,
Could be anywhere,
Any time.

It sneaks up on you
When you're not trying;
You can't ask it in.

It sneaks up on you,
Soft padding paws
Silent as sunshine.

It sneaks up on you
Silky and soothing
And special.

It sneaks up on you
And nuzzles up
So near you notice.

The contentment creature
Always wants to share your life.
If only you'd let it stay.

Happy Days

Days go happy suddenly,
You never know how -
Like the sun coming out
So everything goes bright
And warm as laughter.

After a morning misfortune,
You still never know.
Even after a rotten row
Or a terrible telling-off,
It still can happen.

Seems it's best to look away -
You never can watch.
No use trying too hard;
It's a magic spell
You have to trust.

And if you had the recipe
You could never use it,
Not for yourself on purpose.
It needs something you can't fake:
It needs surprise.

Light pool

Silvery specks float
in the sunlight shafts
shining through the window
onto the bedroom floor,
spotlighting toys, models,
in a clutter of clothes,
pens, crayons, papers,
you forgot to put away.

Somehow now
muddle doesn't matter.
The house is hushed and bright.
The sunlight tidies
and makes it all right seeming.
You can watch, dreaming,
feeling the sunny glow
of just being you.
It's OK to stare.

On the line

On the line in the yard,
The wind makes the washing talk
In sign language.

My shirt is waving its arms wildly
At two vests and some knickers,
Whilst some jeans are kicking
Like footballers warming up
And a sweatshirt is twisting
Towards some shorts,
As if whispering a secret sideways.

The big sheets billow flag-style,
Warning the socks in semaphore
About me, the spy, watching.

Yeah but

Yeah but, you've got to see it's not my fault.
I didn't do it, I didn't mean to,
It was an accident, it just happened, right?
I just didn't know it was going to go wrong.
That's the way it is.

Yeah but, OK I know I was careless,
But trust me, I'm telling you, just listen up!
It's one of those things, stuff happens, all right?
It's a wicked old world, you have to accept it.
That's the way it is.

Yeah but, OK so why blame me?
It isn't fair. So my hand slipped
And just maybe I should have controlled it,
But it wasn't me, I didn't do it.
That's the way it is.

Yeah but, I couldn't help it if my legs let me down.
I mean, they just started running before I knew it.
And I would have stayed to own up
But it wouldn't have been fair when it wasn't my fault?
That's the way it is.

Yeah but, OK so you took the rap.
Someone has to, you know what *they're* like.
OK so I owe you one, I won't forget.
You better believe it, I don't tell porkies.
That's the way it is.

Vincent the Voice

(Song lyric)

There was nothing wrong with Vince
Except his voice - it made you wince.
It was so loud, it made you want to run for cover.
Vincent's very slightest whisper
Deafened unsuspecting listeners
And made tough guys run for comfort to their mothers.
If he began to sing, then all the birds took to the wing
And the dogs would put their snouts up and just howl.
And if he were to shout,
He'd blow your eardrums inside out
And frighten bogeymen right off the prowl.

Vincent! VINCENT!
Vincent the incredible voice

Once when Vince was sleeping,
A burglar came a-creeping,
Wearing a striped jersey and a mask.
Vincent, in his dreaming,
Saw a monster, started screaming
Just as that thief began his thieving task.
Well the burglar was so scared
That he soon had pure white hair
And, when Vincent gave an ear-splitting snore,
He was so frightened by the din
That he jumped out of his skin
And his skeleton went sprinting out the door!

Vincent! VINCENT!
Vincent the incredible voice

When the giant came to town,
He was knocking houses down,
He was big and bold and ugly as a toad.
He'd a club with spikes of iron
And he roared just like a lion
As he squashed the knights who met him on the road.
But when our Vincent sneezed,
The giant was trembling at the knees,
You could see him start to shiver and to shake.
Then Vince, with a megaphone,
Rattled all his giant bones
And made him go and jump into the lake.

Vincent! VINCENT!
Vincent the incredible voice

Well, the mayor made a speech;
He said that Vincent was a peach,
The very greatest hero in the land.
And, for his vocal rescue,
Pinned a medal to his chest too
And everybody cheered and Vince felt grand.
But when he tried to speak,
Vincent blushed from toe to cheek -
He was shy! To talk in public gave him trouble.
When he finally thanked the crowd,
Well, his voice came out so loud
That soon the town was just a pile of rubble.

Vincent! VINCENT!
Vincent the incredible voice

SORRY ABOUT THE NEXT POEM
(IF YOU CAN CALL IT A POEM!).
ROB SNEAKED IT IN AT THE LAST MINUTE.
HE ACTUALLY ADMITTED IT'S REALLY ABOUT
DADS FOR DADS BY A DAD. HE SAYS IT MAKES
FUN OF SOME DADS, BUT IT ALSO MAKES QUITE A
GOOD EXCUSE FOR DADS IN GENERAL AT THE END.
HE SAYS IN FACT THEY HAVE QUITE A HARD
TIME OF IT! THAT DOESN'T MAKE SENSE TO
ME, BUT I'M GOING TO SHOW IT TO MY DAD
AND SEE WHAT HE SAYS. MAYBE YOU
COULD FIND OUT WHAT YOURS
THINKS OF IT TOO.

Dads' dislikes

Theo's dad dislikes waiting outside the school -
You can see he thinks he looks a fool,
Standing with all the women,
Gossiping about school and gyms and slimming;
You can see him glance at his watch, humming
To himself bravely till he sees his son coming
At last. He groans when he's late;
There's already quite enough on his plate,
What with work problems and all.
He's buries himself in a mobile call.

Dinah's dad dislikes the way his daughter slinks
Through her spare time in grown-up fashions; he thinks
She should still be in ribbons and bows,
Not saving for tickets to stadium rock shows.
There's nothing he can do of course,
Except regret not affording the horse
She wanted last year: it would have been simple
Compared to the boys with quiffs and pimples
He imagines will be calling soon.
She might never have listened to wild tunes.

Emily's dad dislikes idle chatter;
He likes to get to the point - it doesn't matter
If it seems rude. The thought of endless stuff
About stuff is more than enough
To drive him crazy, which is a shame –
He sometimes misses spectacular flames.
Emily likes nothing better than talk
(Or, as he puts it, taking her tongue for a walk),
But sometimes her words burn with bright glory:
It's not just natter; it's a fascinating story.

Jack's dad dislikes looking older.
That's why his clothes get bolder and bolder,
What with red jackets and shirts in turquoisy greens;
And his favourite banana yellow jeans:
Which is sad if you know about fashion,
Which he doesn't – his main passion
Is football and cars and watching the news
And expressing his very expert views
On anything and everything and particularly Jack,
Then getting upset when he answers him back.

Most dads dislike the patronizing tones
Teenage offspring use on personal phones
When speaking to them like curious creatures
Who seem to know less than even their teachers
And never were young, don't know what it's like
Having staff who expect you to hang out then hike.
They'd prefer a chauffeur who doesn't complain
And opens the wallet again and again
And smiles when you turn up especially late,
Never breathing bad words about having to wait.

'Dads' and 'dislikes': the two words go together
Like 'England' and 'winter' and 'rainy bad weather':
So it's not all the time, but sometimes it seems so
When they're off on a rant about things that they deem so
Ridiculous or crazy or crass or absurd
That they have to say so in very loud words.
They do have excuses; they may seem like fools,
But they once were young guys who liked to look cool.
So being seen as old now cuts like a knife.
Most Dads dislike not always liking life

THE WEIRD LANGUAGE OF PARENTS CAN BE BAFFLING AS A SPY CODE. YOU TRY TO MAKE IT MAKE SENSE AND YOU END UP TELLING YOURSELF A STORY. I SUPPOSE I DID THAT A LOT WHEN I WAS SMALLER. IT MADE THESE STRANGE PICTURES IN MY MIND — WHICH KIND OF BRINGS ME BACK TO WHERE THESE POEMS STARTED.

Dark horses and Black Sheep

They said that Dave was 'a dark horse'.
I didn't know what it meant
Because the photo was of a man.
Perhaps he was a shape shifter;
Perhaps he knew the way to change
So he got hooves for hands.
Maybe it happened at night.

Then Jo – they called her 'a black sheep',
Though her hair was honey-coloured
And she wore lipstick red as raspberry Ribena
And wasn't woolly and white.
But when she sang the blues
And dad wobbled and wailed on harmonica,
I could almost hear the bleating.

There were others too:
'Greedy pigs' were easy to spot
By their snouts and fat bellies.
'Bit of a bitch': a lady like a mean dog.
Or 'snakes in the grass': it was in their eyes;
Or 'foxy types': they had cunning noses
And 'cows' had hairstyles like horns.

Now I'm older, it makes different sense:
It seems Dave had this scheme that won money,
So one day he walked out on his job
And went to live in Spain.
Jo didn't follow the rules
And got kicked out of a posh school
And the rest were just insults.

All the same, when I finally met Dave last week,
I was on the lookout for kicking hooves
And that swishing mane and tail.
I somehow still expect Aunty Jo to eat grass
Then lift her head and baa.
And often too, I've glimpsed something stranger:
A whole zoo hidden inside people.

TWO FAMILY
TALL TALES

THIS IS A STORY MY UNCLE HENRY TOLD ME WHEN HE CAME TO VISIT ONCE. HE GREW UP IN A VILLAGE IN THE COUNTRY AND HAS QUITE A LOT OF STORIES TO TELL. I'M NOT SURE I BELIEVE ALL OF THEM, BUT I LIKE JUST LISTENING AND IMAGINING. HE HAS A BURRY SORT OF VOICE THAT MAKES YOU FEEL QUITE NICE AND CALM. AS MUCH AS THE STORIES AND THE FUNNY THINGS HE CLAIMS REALLY DID HAPPEN WAY BACK WHEN HE WAS A BOY, I LIKE DREAMING ABOUT THE DAYS WHEN YOU WERE ALLOWED TO GO OFF WANDERING ALL DAY WITH YOUR FRIENDS IN THE WOODS AND OVER FIELDS, THE WAY MY UNCLE SAYS IT USED TO BE WHEN HE WAS MY AGE.

I would have been eleven at the time - eleven and about four months. I know that because it was the summer holidays. We were out in the woods. There was my brother Jack, my friend Pete and me and we found this egg. It was bigger than any egg we'd seen before - and, being country kids, we had seen a few big eggs. Ducks' eggs were big, goose eggs were bigger, swans' eggs could be very big, but this was larger still, almost the size of an ostrich egg I'd seen in a museum once. It was pale green with darker green blotches and it was still warm, as if it had just been laid or had maybe just tumbled out of the nest from under its mother.

Once we'd felt the warmth, we began to hunt around. Maybe the nest was somewhere nearby, up in a tree perhaps. Maybe we could find it and put the egg back. But if there was a nest, we could find not one single sign of it.

Maybe the mother bird herself was somewhere around, amongst the trees. We hid and watched and waited, but we couldn't get any sense at all of a large bird anywhere nearby, just the cawing of rooks and the cooing of pigeons. In the end we decided that we would have to take it home. Pete and his dad had bred budgies for a while and he still had the equipment. We reckoned we could put the egg safely in their shed - they had an incubator his dad had rigged up. Once it was in that, we should be able to do a more thorough hunt, find the nest or the mother and return the strange egg.

We never did find either the nest or the mother. Events took over. It must have been the heat that brought it on. The egg cracked and, slowly, slowly, George hatched out - we called him that straight away, I can't remember why. It was a real thrill, seeing him come out - gradually pushing his way out and shoving the bits of eggshell away. We decided he must be a boy - even though he was a gawky little chick with the egg yolk still smeared on his goose-pimply skin and scarcely a feather on him as yet. There was the hint of a scarlet crest on the top of his puckered little head and a cocky sort of air to him that suggested a barnyard rooster.

Mind you, I say little but George was never really small. He looked surprisingly big even then, sitting there under the glow of the infra-red lamp - once the legs that must have been curled up inside that shell unknotted themselves, once he began to totter around cautiously, very ungainly and uncertain. I remember saying to Pete that you would never have believed there was so much bird inside that eggshell, large though it was.

During the days and the weeks that followed, that chick grew quickly. It was a good job Pete had quite a bit of seed left over from the budgie hobby, because George had a big appetite. Apart from the millet and the barley, he developed an odd taste for raspberry jam. Pete's dad grew a lot of his own fruit and vegetables and his mum was into making jam. There were stacks of it in carefully labelled jars down one side of the shed. Sometime around a week into his stay, we discovered that George loved the stuff. He couldn't get enough of it. I think we'd opened a jar and put some on his dish, just for a joke and to see what would happen and he had gobbled it up, giving one of his strange strangled squawks that meant something like, 'More please!' It always had to be the raspberry - he didn't care for greengage or plumb or even strawberry jam. It was a good job they'd had a bumper crop of raspberries the previous season, so there was plenty of it.

How we managed to keep George a secret for so long, I do not know. We were in the midst of the balmy, hot days of the long summer holidays and we had plenty of time on our hands - children didn't get these long holidays abroad or spend their time on courses in those days. We used to take him out once he'd grown bigger. We always got him away in the early morning and smuggled him back in the evening, as it was getting dark. We just knew that the adults wouldn't approve; they would insist we took him to a zoo and we didn't want that, because we were having fun and George was too.

He was turning into a strange looking bird and no

mistake, the kind of creature you would expect to see in a jungle or maybe a wild life park, rather than in an ordinary English village with thatched cottages and a village green. That's why we kept him in the woods by day, at a secret camp we had there. By this time, he was as big as a turkey and the feathers on him were turning to a lurid lime green, with that scarlet crest and a streak of scarlet shading to orange down each wing. Sometimes he would flap those wings at the end of his lead, as if he meant business – we had him on a lead you see, with an old dog collar my black Labrador, Mango, had worn when she was a puppy. It still had her name printed on a metal panel fixed to the leather. To this we had attached a length of rope you could pay out and lengthen when there was the space for him to poke around a bit – birds like that do seem to want to poke around in the undergrowth. He was probably finding worms and bugs to eat.

I think we'd had him nearly a month when he flew for the first time. In the middle of the woods, there was a clearing that was grassy and open, so we'd let him wander on the end of his rope. He was flapping around in a way we'd seen him do before. It hadn't occurred to us that he would ever actually take off, because he was so big. Flying didn't seem likely, but he did it that day. It took us several seconds for me to realise and I was on the other end of the rope - it was my turn to hold him. He took a little run, flailing around wildly with his clumsy wings. I was so used to him doing that sort of thing that I hardly noticed, until the rope went tight and I saw that he was up in the air. He flew in a circle and then his usual squawk came out – except that it was not the usual one, because it wasn't strangled and quiet any more, but big and full and throaty. Just for an instant as he landed in a tangle of rope, I fancied I heard an answer somewhere in the woods, but it might have been an echo.

He did it every time after that - every time we were out in the woods in the clearing and sometimes on the way home too. He got very good at it, so good he almost pulled you off the ground as he soared upwards. Had he stayed with us, I'm sure he would have done just that, because he went on growing till he was almost the size of a small emu – a green emu with long orange legs and big wings. Of course memory exaggerate things and I was not particularly big myself at the time, so he might have seemed bigger than he was, but he was certainly big enough for Louis to sit astride.

Louis was a little boy, about four or five, and he followed us whenever he could, the way some little children do - whenever he could get away from his mum, whenever we couldn't get away from him. We were always kind enough to him I think - we talked to him and teased him gently in the way you do with little children. But then of course we wanted to be off and get on with whatever we were doing. We hadn't told him about George and we wouldn't have meant to do anything of the kind. Louis was just there one day, just when we were taking George back. I don't know how he came to be out at that time, but in those days parents used to allow children to roam a lot more than they do now and he was roaming near the place where he lived. We came face to face with him as we came out of the woods. He looked at

George and his eyes went enormous – you know, the way they always describe them in books, like saucers; they really seemed that big. 'What's that?' he said in that high, squeaky little voice that could at times be so irritating – like now, when we had a secret we just knew he wouldn't be able to keep.

It must have been a bribe to keep him quiet. We told him that he could ride on George and we lifted him up and put him on the bird, not really meaning to let go and put his full weight on the poor creature, but sometimes things don't work out the way you mean them to. He made a grab for George's neck, and George promptly panicked, leapt and bucked us away, then sprinted off at top speed with poor little Louis clinging on for all he was worth and the rope dangling uselessly behind him. A moment later, they were airborne and Louis was obviously liking it because he went: 'Weeeeee!' just as if he was on a slide or a fairground ride.

Who knows what would have happened if he'd stayed on? Maybe he'd have flown away to Timbuktu and the Sahara desert on George, but he lost his hold and tumbled off before they had gone much above head height. Then there were the howls and shrieks as he landed and, for a moment, we were too busy attending to a hurt little boy to notice George flying up and up and up. When we did look, he was way above the trees, giving his deep, chirring, purring squawk. Then, suddenly, to our total amazement, we not only heard an answering cry but we actually saw another one, half again as big. It must have been his mum or dad. It joined him there in the air and led him away, off over the woods and beyond.

We watched in a daze as they flew away and, do you know, I never ever saw them again. But here's the funny thing. I know that the rope we had on George came away because I saw it happen some time before we lost sight of him and we actually found it in the woods the next day, but there was definitely no collar attached. That must have stayed on him. It was years later, not so very long ago in fact, that I found that collar. At the time, I was at the top of a mountain in Morocco and there it was, looking sun-bleached and weathered of course, because it must have been on the rock where I found it for ages. Somehow I just knew it had to be the same collar because it had 'Mango' on a rectangular tin plate attached to the leather. I've never worked out how it got there. But anyway, I've got that collar at home and I'll show it to you one day, then you'll know that this story's true.'

WHEN HE CAME TO VISIT AGAIN, UNCLE HENRY KEPT HIS PROMISE AND SHOWED ME THE COLLAR. IT REALLY DID HAVE A RECTANGULAR TIN PLATE WITH THE NAME, 'MANGO' VERY CLEARLY ENGRAVED. IT ALSO LOOKED AS THOUGH IT COULD HAVE BEEN OUT IN THE HOT SUN AND THE FREEZING COLD SNOW FOR QUITE A LONG TIME — WHICH I SUPPOSE ALL PROVED THAT THE STORY WAS AT LEAST A BIT TRUE.

Will's New Suit

THIS IS ONE OF ROB'S FAMILY TALL TALES. THERE IS THIS STORY ON HIS WILL'S CLOGS CD WHICH REALLY MAKES ME LAUGH. IT'S ALL ABOUT HIS LANCASHIRE GREAT GREAT GRANDAD AND THE BAD LUCK THIS HUGE, STINKY PAIR OF CLOGS BROUGHT HIM AND HOW IT TURNED OUT QUITE WELL IN THE END. I ASKED ROB IF THERE WERE ANY MORE LIKE THAT AND HE TOLD ME THIS ONE, WHICH IS ABOUT THE SAME MAN ONLY YEARS LATER. HE WROTE IT DOWN FOR ME AND SAID HE'D DONE IT IN STORYTELLING STYLE RATHER THAN IN 'BOOK LANGUAGE'. HE SAID THAT'S WHY IT QUITE OFTEN SLIPS INTO THE PRESENT TENSE - APPARENTLY STORYTELLERS OFTEN DO THAT WHEN THEY'RE SPEAKING. HE TOLD ME TO TRY TO IMAGINE THE VERY BROAD LANCASHIRE ACCENTS OF THE CHARACTERS WHEN I READ IT ON THE PAGE - WHICH WAS QUITE HARD, BECAUSE I DON'T ACTUALLY LIVE IN LANCASHIRE MYSELF AND I'VE ONLY HEARD ROB DOING HIS IMITATIONS, WHICH ARE PROBABLY WRONG. ANYWAY HE SAID HE HAD SUGGESTED A BIT OF THAT IN THE WAY HE DID THEIR WORDS, THOUGH HE RECKONED THAT IF HE WROTE IT ALL THE WAY THEY'D HAVE SAID IT, NOT MANY WOULD UNDERSTAND - AND HE WASN'T SURE HE WOULD EITHER. WHICH WAS A WEIRD THING TO SAY REALLY.

After all the fuss with the clogs, Will Bond re-built his fortunes and then he married Liza, my great great grandmother. They had a good life and a long one. One time, when all the children had grown up and they were getting on in years, Liza and her friend Nell were sitting at the kitchen table and having a good old gossip over a cup of tea. Liza looks and Nell and she says, 'Now my Will, 'e's a lovely man , but 'e's a bit trusting, tha knows. He always believes stuff 'e's told. I reckon if you told 'im it were Monday when it were Tuesday and you told him often enough, 'e'd believe you.'

'Aye!' laughs Nell, 'my Ernest, 'e's the same. If you were to tell 'im it were night time in t' middle of day and if you told 'im well enough, 'e'd be in 'is nightshirt next thing.'

'Aye, but Will's worse. If you told 'im black were white, 'e'd believe it.'

'Aye, but Ernie... well, if you told 'im it were summer when it were winter, 'e'd be putting on his winter woollies in no time...'

It went on like that for a while and it started to get just a bit competitive - in fact, more than a bit competitive in the finish, because they decided to have a contest. They'd take a week and see who could make their husbands believe the daftest thing and do the stupidest thing. That's how it all began.

Now Liza went home and she made her preparations. She got out two knitting needles - no wool, just knitting needles - and she waited till Will came in. When at last he did, she was there in her armchair by the fire, clicking those needles together for all the world as if she were knitting. But no wool as I say.

Will spots this after a while and he says, 'What're you doing love?'

'I'm knitting you a new suit.'

'Knitting a suit? I never 'eard o' that.'

'Oh, it's all the rage,' says Liza. 'I'm gonna do the lot - jacket, trousers, pants, shirt, everything. Just you wait and see.'

'Well that's... um, very nice...' Will hesitates and peers closely at what she's doing. 'But er... don't you, er... well, don't you need some wool or some thread of some kind?'

'Aye, I do... I've got some 'ere. But tell me something, because this is by way of being a test. Can you really not see anything?'

Will had a vague inkling that he should somehow or other be seeing something from the way she said that, though of course he could see no thread at all. So he buys time as they say. 'Oh sorry,' he says, 'I've not got me glasses on at the moment.' He fumbles around looking for his reading specs.

'You see,' Liza goes on, 'this is very special wool I had from a gypsy lady this afternoon. Lovely stuff it is, the very best, I knew that straight away. But those travelling folk know a thing or two and she did say something when I bought it. 'Course I didn't believe her at the time, but I'm beginning to wonder now. She told me, "If your husband's in the habit of telling you lies, he won't be able to see this wool at all." Apparently it has a sort of magic to it, see. Have you been telling me lies, Will Bond?'

Now Will had told the odd little fib here and there - about why he'd been in late perhaps, pretending he'd been working on the top field when he'd been in the pub, that sort of thing. He knew that and Liza knew it too. They both told their little untruths now and then and that's a thing a lot of people do, in the family especially. Another thing a lot of people do is not to admit it, not most of the time. Will certainly wasn't about to admit it now anyway, so he made a big show of putting on his glasses and peering across at the knitting. 'Oh yes... I see,' he says. 'Very nice. What... er... colour would you say it was?'

'Well what colour would you say it was?'

'Oh...ummm... well, greenish... with a bit of, um, brown and ermmm...'

Will did his best to pretend he could see the thread and Liza let him struggle until she was ready for her next move. 'Right, this sleeve is ready. We'd best try it on you.' She held something that wasn't there at all up against his arm, as if trying to decide whether the length was right. So Will dutifully tried this something that wasn't there on and agreed that it was just about how it should be.

The trouble with pretending is knowing when to stop, because the more you pretend something, the more real it seems to be, until it's hard to remember you're pretending at all. That's the way of things. To begin with I suppose Will more or less knew he was just going along with it all to keep Liza happy and it didn't seem too important. But she wasn't planning to stop; she went on and on with it. Later than night he had to try on another sleeve and the next day the whole jacket.... then it was the shirt ... and the waistcoat and the trousers... and the vest and the pants. Every day there was bit more until, when the week was almost over, she claimed it was all done and complete. By this time, Will truly was seeing this something that wasn't there. He'd imagined it all so well that he genuinely felt as though he was putting on a real suit.

You see, he'd convinced himself that he didn't tell lies, not really big ones, not lies that really mattered. But when he put the whole suit on, he was stark naked. That was the fact of the matter - the bare truth if you like.

Meanwhile, Nell was up to her own kinds of tricks with her husband, Ernest. That very first evening, whilst Liza was doing her stuff with the knitting needles, this is what had happened. Ernie walks in the door and she takes one look at him and she says, 'What's up love? Tha's like death warmed up.'

'Me?' says Ernie. 'I'm fine. Never felt better.'

'Well, I don't know.' Nelly shakes her head. 'Tha looks pretty poorly to me. Better come over 'ere by t' fire...'

Ernie goes on protesting that he feels all right for a while, but the doubts start to creep into his mind. She makes him look in the mirror, insisting that he looks very pale. In fact he does look pale - probably because of the way the lamp's placed, probably because he often looks pale anyway, but he doesn't think of that. Anyway, she keeps on and on about him looking bad, tells him he'd better stick to a light supper, ushers him off to bed early and treats him in every way as though he's really ill. So of course he even starts to feel ill. It can work like that. Someone makes out you're ill and somehow you start to believe them, even if you thought you were feeling great. It can work the other way round too when someone tells you you're well, which is good I suppose.

But as for Ernie, Nelly wasn't about to tell him he was well because she'd got her plan worked out. She'd had a little word with her brother, who was a funeral director and had plenty of coffins to spare. He was in on the plot, you'll see how in a minute or two. The next day she wouldn't allow Ernie to go

85

out to do his work - she'd sorted that one out on the side too, being canny about such things, telling people he was taking a holiday and actually arranging for him to have a few days off he was owed. She made him stay in bed day after day, keeping him on invalid's food - chicken broth and bread and water and the like. Poor old Ernie was feeling worse and worse until finally Nelly walks into the spare bedroom where she's got him lying and she screams, 'Oh no, 'e's dead! You poor old chap!' She bursts into floods of fake tears.

He lies there thinking, 'Oh dear, I'm dead. So this is 'ow it feels. I'd best not try and move.' Nelly is making a big show of grief and she goes and gets pennies and puts them over his eyes like they used to in those days. Then she gets her brother to come and sort him out and soon she's got the funeral organized and Ernie is in the coffin, lying there thinking, 'Mustn't budge. Don't want to frighten folk.' Nelly has had invitations written out to quite a few people, asking them to come along to the church specially. Of course, most of them are in on the act, because they'd be very upset otherwise. But the undertaker's men, who would carry the coffin - they hadn't the foggiest notion of the trick they were taking part in. She wanted it all to seem real you see.

One of the people to get an invitation was my great great grandfather, Will Bond. It arrived just as he was trying on his new suit, the whole lot. He'd just taken off all his clothes and put the new ones on, the shirt and the pants and the vest and the waistcoat and the jacket and the trousers. Just for a moment, he had looked at himself and thought, 'Oh no! I'm not wearing a stitch!' But then he'd explained it to himself: 'That's because of those lies I used to tell! I've given that up now.' When he'd said that, he had seen the suit very clearly again. It looked all very posh, very fashionable - he had an excellent imagination.

Then the card arrived, telling him to come down to the church at once if he would. He looks at it and he says, 'Poor old Ernie! I were only talking to him last week and he looked fine. Oh dearie me... I'll have to go down there. What shall I wear?'

'Why, your new suit of course,' says Liza. She knew what the game was and she wasn't going to let Nelly get the better of her. 'It looks just lovely! But you can't go in bare feet, can you now? Put your boots on.' You see, by this time, Will could afford boots, not like when the clogs got him into so much trouble in the *Will's Clogs* story. He had two pairs in fact, a brown pair and a black pair. It was the black ones he put on now and then Liza more or less shoved him out into the street.

Will walked along, very proud of his new clothes. He passed a couple of old ladies in the street in the village and they looked at him in horror and screamed, because of course he was in his birthday suit, naked as nature expected - apart from the boots of course. One man he knew shouted out, 'Hey Will Bond, tha should 'ave ironed that shirt before tha put it on!' Another couple of fellows were laughing and jeering and Will was thinking, 'Stupid blighters! Who'd have thought so many people tell lies? They just can't see my suit because of all the fibs they tell!' He walked along with his nose in the air, with a sense of dignity.

Now the sight of a stark naked man in a pair of boots is funny enough, but there's one thing that's much funnier: the sight of a stark naked man walking along the street with a sense of dignity. It was hilarious. The more people laughed, the more Will stood on that dignity - or maybe I should say walked on it. The more he did that, the funnier he looked.

He arrived at the churchyard just as the undertaker's men were lifting the coffin with Ernie inside down from the carriage, onto their shoulders. They walked forward, very slow and respectul, which is what they were paid to do. There they were in their black suits with black hats, carrying the coffin, looking solemn and serious, something they did all the time so they knew just how to do it. But even a man who spends his time looking very solemn and serious and walking slowly and respectfully with a coffin on his shoulders has been a boy once, a boy with the giggles, a boy just caught out for a moment by something unexpected, something so completely silly and ridiculous that it can't help but start the laughter. You know how it happens, little gusts of giggles that start to swell up inside you as you try to hold them back, until you're quivering and shaking and the tears are starting to stream with the effort? Well that's how it was for one of those men with the coffin. He glanced over his shoulder as they went down the path towards the church and he saw... a stark naked man in a pair of boots with his nose in the air. It somehow just hit him, full on somewhere in the stomach and he started to twitch and then to shake. Next one of the other fellows, wondering what was the matter, glanced over and he saw almost exactly the same thing. He started to shake as well, which made it worse because, as a lot of people know, it's much more difficult to stop the giggles if one of your friends is giggling too. Laughter is catching. It certainly caught the third man and he looked and he saw too. The three blokes on the other side couldn't see what they could see, but they just sensed the chuckles and the shakes and that was almost as bad. That coffin on all their shoulders was soon shaking up and down like a boat on big waves, with Ernie inside thinking, 'Whatever's going on.' He completely forgot for a moment he was supposed to be dead and shoved the lid of the coffin up to have a look.

There was a loud shriek of terror from some startled girls who'd been watching. The men looked up and dropped the coffin and made a run for it, thinking it was a ghost or something. Ernie jumped up in his grave clothes, looking like a mummy from some horror film and he remembers he's supposed to be dead, so he chases after the men to remind them they're supposed to be burying him today. And Will... well, he takes one look at the undertaker's men running towards him and he turns on his heels and runs away, just as fast as he can go, thinking they're after his new suit.

All the people in the street are laughing away at this strange procession of runners - a man in grave clothes screaming, 'I'm dead. Come on now, you've to bury me!', six men in black suits, their black hats tumbling off as they ran away, and a stark naked man, sprinting along in a pair of boots.

Anyway, now you can decide for yourself who won the competition: who, in fact, was the daftest. I'll run through the cast of characters in this story. Do you reckon it was Liza or Nelly who set the whole thing up? Maybe not as they were obviously very scheming and cunning. But it might have been the people who watched and screamed or screeched with laughter. Or the undertakers men, running away from what they thought was a ghost? But, if I'm being serious, I'd guess you would think it was either Ernie, who thought he was dead when he'd only to pinch himself to know that he was alive, or my great great grandfather, Will Bond, who walked through the street wearing nothing at all but a pair of boots and a sense of dignity.

But there are other people involved in the tale and I should mention them too. It takes more than characters to make a story; readers or listeners have to be involved as well. So maybe it was you, the reader who was the daftest for reading such an absurd, ridiculous and impossible tale. Or then again, maybe the daftest of all was me for writing it down and putting it in a book.

I don't know. All I know is that this story's done now and so is the book and it's all just as true as I could make it.

The song lyrics in this book have been taken from two CDs

The Wonderful Store - Strange, fantastical & ridiculous songs by Rob Parkinson (Imaginary Journeys 1989 & 2003)

Wild Imaginings - Weird, wacky & wild songs by Rob Parkinson (Imaginary Journeys 2003)

Both are available from **www.imaginaryjourneys.co.uk**

The story CD *Will's Clogs - Unlikely & fantastical tales* with Rob Parkinson (Imaginary Journeys 1991 & 2003) includes the original tall tale mentioned in *Will's New Suit* and is also available for the same source or from book dealers.

Also available by Rob Parkinson:

For all ages:
Fabulous Fables - Witty & wise tales from world traditions with Rob Parkinson (CD) - Imaginary Journeys 2008

For adults:

Audio:
Powerful Stories (Double CD) - Uncommon Knowledge 2003
*Just Imagine (*CD) - Imaginary Journeys 2005

Books:
Storytelling & Imagination (Beyond basic literacy 8 - 14) (Routledge 2010)
Transforming Tales (How stories can change people) (Jessica Kingsley 2009)

For adults & children:

The Natural Storytellers booklet series from Imaginary Journeys:
Tall Tale Telling (24 fun games for making & telling incredible stories) - 2004
Imagine On (24 fun ways to picture & tell marvellous stories) - 2005
Yarn Spinning (24 fun ways to stretch a tale in the telling) - 2007
New Lamps from Old (24 fun games for making tales from old plots) - 2007

All available from Imaginary Journeys (see above) or from book dealers.